To Severin:
Welcome To The World! We're so
Glad That you're Here. You Are Magic!

Love,
Ivy

On the day that we met and I put you to bed,
I noticed a crown on the top of your head.

It was made up of sparkling, glimmering things
like moonlight and fireflies, and dragonfly wings.

The Crown on Your Head

Nancy Tillman

FEIWEL AND FRIENDS
NEW YORK

As the days came and went,
it was faithful and true...

. . . and it grew right along with the rest of you.

I always knew just what your crown meant.
It said that you were MAGNIFICENT.

(That means you are grand from your toes to your chin.
Take a deep breath, and let that sink in.)

That's about as high as a word can climb!
That's the top of a mountain . . .
a steeple chime.

That's over the moon in a nursery rhyme . . .

and it means, like a star,

YOU WERE BORN TO SHINE.

(Blink three times and . . . there you are!
You are *twinkling*, little star!)

In other words, from your very first day,
you were chosen to glow in a very big way!

With your crown made of glittering, high-flying things,
you've got wind in your pocket, your wishes have wings.

You can run like you mean it . . . so, let the wind blow. . . .

There's just no telling how high you can go!

Whatever it is you choose to do,
no one can do it exactly like you.
Ride on the big slide! And if you fall down,
remember your glorious, marvelous crown.

It won't flicker or fade. It won't dim. It won't leave.

ALL YOU HAVE TO DO IS BELIEVE.

Do you, my child? I hope that you do.
The world is a wonderland waiting for you.

And you get to share it with all your friends, too!
They *each* have a crown that is faithful and true.

No one's is brighter, no one's is duller.

It's only a crown of a different color.

So sometimes, just every now and then, whisper "I believe" again.
Your crown is your best friend forever, by far.

It tells the true story of just who you are.

That's why every night, when I put you to bed,
I'm careful to kiss the crown on your head.

A Note From Your Crown

I'm made out of magic most people can't see
(which is really quite clever, if you should ask me).
But if ever you're worried and really must know,
you can tell that I'm there by the warmth of my glow.

Press your hand to the top of your head.
Feel me? Okay. Put your worries to bed.

A Feiwel and Friends Book
An Imprint of Macmillan

Printed in May 2011 in China by South China Printing Co. Ltd., Dongguan City, Guangdong Province.
For information, address Feiwel and Friends, 175 Fifth Avenue, New York, N.Y. 10010.

Library of Congress Cataloging-in-Publication Data Available

ISBN: 978-0-312-64521-2

Book design by Rich Deas and Kathleen Breitenfeld

Feiwel and Friends logo designed by Filomena Tuosto

First Edition: 2011

10 9 8 7 6 5 4 3 2 1

mackids.com

You are loved.